Orcish Poetry

S.J. Breier

Thanks for

coming by

Cover Art

Jonathan Nowinski

This book is dedicated to my parents who taught me a love of reading.

Table of Contents

OPEN GAME LICENSE Version 1.0a

The following text is the property of Wizards of the Coast, Inc. and is Copyright 2000 Wizards of the Coast, Inc ("Wizards"). All Rights Reserved.

1. Definitions: (a)"Contributors" means the copyright and/or trademark owners who have contributed Open Game Content; (b)"Derivative Material" means copyrighted material including derivative works and translations (including into other computer languages), potation, modification, correction, addition, extension, upgrade, improvement, compilation, abridgment or other form in which an existing work may be recast, transformed or adapted; (c) "Distribute" means to reproduce, license, rent, lease, sell, broadcast, publicly display, transmit or otherwise distribute; (d)"Open Game Content" means the game mechanic and includes the methods, procedures, processes

and routines to the extent such content does not embody the Product Identity and is an enhancement over the prior art and any additional content clearly identified as Open Game Content by the Contributor, and means any work covered by this License, including translations and derivative works under copyright law, but specifically excludes Product Identity. (e) "Product Identity" means product and product line names, logos and identifying marks including trade dress; artifacts; creatures characters; stories, storylines, plots, thematic elements, dialogue, incidents, language, artwork, symbols, designs, depictions, likenesses, formats, poses, concepts, themes and graphic, photographic and other visual or audio representations; names and descriptions of characters, spells, enchantments, personalities, teams, personas, likenesses and special abilities; places, locations, environments, creatures, equipment, magical or supernatural abilities or effects, logos, symbols, or graphic designs; and any other trademark or registered trademark clearly identified as Product identity by the owner of the Product Identity, and which specifically excludes the Open Game Content; (f) "Trademark" means the logos, names, mark, sign, motto, designs that are used by a Contributor to identify itself or its products or the associated products contributed to the Open Game License by the Contributor (g) "Use", "Used" or "Using" means to use, Distribute, copy, edit, format, modify, translate and otherwise create Derivative Material of Open Game Content. (h) "You" or "Your" means the licensee in terms of this agreement.

2. The License: This License applies to any Open Game Content that contains a notice indicating that the Open Game Content may only be Used under and in terms of this License. You must affix such a notice to any Open Game Content that you Use. No terms may be added to or subtracted from this License except as described by the License itself. No other terms or conditions may be applied

to any Open Game Content distributed using this License.

3.Offer and Acceptance: By Using the Open Game Content You indicate Your acceptance of the terms of this License.

4. Grant and Consideration: In consideration for agreeing to use this License, the Contributors grant You a perpetual, worldwide, royalty-free, non-exclusive license with the exact terms of this License to Use, the Open Game Content.

5.Representation of Authority to Contribute: If You are contributing original material as Open Game Content, You represent that Your Contributions are Your original creation and/or You have sufficient rights to grant the rights conveyed by this License.

6.Notice of License Copyright: You must update the COPYRIGHT NOTICE portion of this License to include the exact text of the COPYRIGHT NOTICE of any Open Game Content You are copying, modifying or distributing, and You must add the title, the copyright date, and the copyright holder's name to the COPYRIGHT NOTICE of any original Open Game Content you Distribute.

7. Use of Product Identity: You agree not to Use any Product Identity, including as an indication as to compatibility, except as expressly licensed in another, independent Agreement with the owner of each element of that Product Identity. You agree not to indicate compatibility or co-adaptability with any Trademark or Registered Trademark in conjunction with a work containing Open Game Content except as expressly licensed in another, independent Agreement with the owner of such Trademark or Registered Trademark. The use of any Product Identity in Open Game Content does not constitute a challenge to the ownership of that Product Identity. The owner of any Product Identity used in Open Game Content

shall retain all rights, title and interest in and to that Product Identity.

8. Identification: If you distribute Open Game Content You must clearly indicate which portions of the work that you are distributing are Open Game Content.

9. Updating the License: Wizards or its designated Agents may publish updated versions of this License. You may use any authorized version of this License to copy, modify and distribute any Open Game Content originally distributed under any version of this License.

10 Copy of this License: You MUST include a copy of this License with every copy of the Open Game Content You Distribute.

11. Use of Contributor Credits: You may not market or

advertise the Open Game Content using the name of any Contributor unless You have written permission from the Contributor to do so.

12. Inability to Comply: If it is impossible for You to comply with any of the terms of this License with respect to some or all of the Open Game Content due to statute, judicial order, or governmental regulation then You may not Use any Open Game Material so affected.

13 Termination: This License will terminate automatically if You fail to comply with all terms herein and fail to cure such breach within 30 days of becoming aware of the breach. All sublicenses shall survive the termination of this License.

14 Reformation: If any provision of this License is held to be unenforceable, such provision shall be reformed only to the extent necessary to make it enforceable.

15 COPYRIGHT NOTICE

Introduction

If you are looking for a story of heroes, bright and strong, or brooding and contemplative, close this book and see if you can find one on the other side of the shelf. Where there are heroes there are villains, and this is the story of the latter. If your curiosity beckons you, welcome, read on, learn of this darkness. Whether you are interested in unveiling the shadow of your own self, or if you are in search of an enemy worthy of heroes on their path of destiny, you will find within, orcs described through their own poetry. As a translator of orcish poetry I have had a lot of explaining to do. I'll meet someone new and tell them I'm working on a fantasy poetry project. It's about orcs. I ask them if they know what orcs are, and some break into a smile, but many give me a blank look. I try for the closest cultural reference, which is The Lord of the Rings trilogy. Still, often I get the blank look, and I have to describe scenes from the movies to jar some memories of those orc soldiers. Reader, I hope you do know what orcs are, but if not I hope you find pleasure in discovering their soul. Orcs are grey-green monsters with only a brute intelligence, and a longing for violence. Even so, they have a depth of sorts, a culture, and a body of poetry. With great difficulty have I gathered this knowledge. Orcs are given to killing strangers who would walk in their midst. Often enough orcs kill one another. They are uncomfortable sharing any of their poetic musings with outsiders. Nevertheless I have succeeded in returning from the orc lands with a good amount of their poetry.

After my training in Anthropology, I have translated it for human eyes. Please understand the painstaking process of finding the right English words to convey the blunt, barbarous, and often stupid language of the orcs, without losing any of its innate rhythm, poetry, or bloodthirsty rage. Orcs have 24 words for impale, and 32 different adverbs to be used with 'bash with club.' Due to their stupidity they often forget many of these words, and so sometimes have less to work with, or they create other new words on the spot. Orcs make grammatical errors as a rule, and getting all their spelling correct is considered 'elfie' or trying to look too good. As a translator, working with a language that is not my own, it takes a great deal to stay on top of their poetry.

In presenting orcish poetry I often get the question, "Who are these orcs?" The best way to find out is to read their poetry. A good second reference is the Wikipedia, which has an entry for orc along with everything else. If you want a quicker reference, try the Dictionary. The one on my computer came up with an informative result.

If you really like dictionaries though, you should have a look at the Oxford English Dictionary. It's the ally of every scholar, a keepsake of Anthropologists in the specialization of orcish studies. The O.E.D. has three definitions for orc. In Milton's 1667 Paradise Lost 835 “The haunt of Seales and Orcs, and Sea-mews clang.” It's a word related to orca, great cetacean. We see that orc has a long lived meaning, though not the one written of in these poems. The whale meaning of orc has survived as far as 1908 J. Payne Carol & Cadence 148 "The tiger of the sea-deeps knew,—the Orc".

The second use of orc is the contemporary fantasy definition which came of age with the works of J.R.R. Tolkien. It is the one used here. Early use of orc meant monster with its modern use turning to a specific sort of fantasy monster.

The third use of orc is as a verb. It is possible to orc someone. Its meaning is similar to demonize, to make a monster out of. If you read enough of these poems you may be orced, turned into one.

Many readers familiar with the modern fantasy usage of orc want to know if my orcs are J.R.R. Tolkien orcs, D&D orcs, or orcs from some other variegated fantasy literature.

The poems could be applied to any kind of orc, more or less. In the greatest sense these poems were written by everyorc. In the more narrow and specific sense, the poetry is further from orcish roots in J.R.R. Tolkien's work, and closer to the contemporary orc in Dungeons & Dragons and Pathfinder games. As such they may be used as a role aid for RPGs (Roleplaying Games).

The poetry could be used in a game in which the adventurers encounter orcish raiders with an orcish bard. Otherwise a party of adventurers might find them in the library of an archmage with an interest in accumulating many forms of knowledge.

The one system-specific poem is Pomarj Days, as The Pomarj is a geographical location in The World of Greyhawk, whose license belongs to Wizards of the Coast. The Pomarj may also be applied to any area conquered by orcs. In the orcish mind any such land justly belongs to them. I included Wizard's OGL (Open Game License) for Pomarj Days.

Some have raised question to the authenticity of my work, and the more audacious have called me a fraud, proclaiming that I hold the barest of all credentials in Anthropology, and that I know little of orcs or their tongue. My naysayers would have that I did not cross the curtain into the fantasy realm, ventured not across the marshy wastes of Sylanrah, neither did I befriend a nomadic guide to take me across the Fiery Desert of Fetheym, nor did I dwell among the hill tribes of Karndres on my way to the Pomarj. The doubters and those of ill will claim it would have been impossible for me to have made peaceful contact with the orcs. They say that in any case this is immaterial since a translation itself is quite impossible, for there is no orcish poetry, and the orcs have no written mark.

Believe them not, for what follows is my work, carefully drawn from orcish hand, and delivered to you dear reader, for sake of understanding and bridging cultures. The orcs do indeed have a poetry, and there are those among them with a greater spark of intelligence than the others. Do not be surprised if at times they wax on in quite a literate manner. Most of all, enjoy, and when you have finished the work, do not let anyone say to you that you have not read orcish poetry.

On Rock With Pen

The first orc poem

Sit here with pen

Learnt write craft

Secret words for me.

Other Orks not know

Other Orks not see

Crafty Craft Crafting.

They know good slaughter

They know good char

But unknown verse.

Feel good what I do for Orkish heart

Feel good in blood and head

Friends think good, or chop?

Who to share?

Who to know?

Orkness get culture from mark?

On rock with pen

By trees alone

What if turn into Elf?

To Serve Elf

The first Orc poem ever translated

Elfie smash and bleed and gore,
Elfie cry and no more lore,
Singing elfies trickling like brook,
End up as fishies, sword as hook.

Lying elfies rage Orcish swell,
Unlike us, pretty not smell,
In tree homes so dear and elegance refine,
Hate such magikers, on them we dine.

Grating on elfies, like them not,
We Orcies, much prefer rot,
But without elfies, what we do?
Diced, favorite ingredient of stew.

Go Clubbing

When weapons sharpened
and nothing to do
With friends go clubbing

Favorite places
All in Orcs go
Look good while break bone

Bash bash Halfling or who show up
Drinking party brew, we all along
See if attractive female, see if she come along

Carried home from slaughter
Crash all to bed
Waken next noon head ache from club!

Best part in hurt

Such good club

Who club me, girl?

Or girl me club?

Kill – Day

Grr Sng rary sng

A day to kill

no elves to kill

Grind in teeth, last year's bones

Good chew

when so much bad

bad

bad

bad

me bad

village bad

orcs bad

elves good

What it like to be elf?

Is goody-goody dancing in sun climbing tree

happy happy

No good

I stay unhappy, mad

stay orc, stay bad

Kinds of Sausage

Sausage Intestines

run run, on a sausage run

so love the spurting

fire

cook in pot

boiled by ma

or grilled by pa

On long way; sometimes eat raw

not do too often

develop bad habit

sausage - sausage - sausage - Yam!

Mean and Lonely

Lonely is the ork

Among all mean creatures

No one else like

Yarrrgh goes the ork

Kill father maim child

And no one like

Go to human settlement does ork

Burn field, chew on house

But no one like!

It not ork's fault

That he bad, he not try

He simply ork

And okay, sometime he try

Be cruelest and viciousest around,

But that best way, besides ogres mean too

Ork Female I Saw

Warts and all,

Scars over breast, stomach, and thigh – best places,

She gruesome, she reeking, she fiend.

My love kills with axe,

Heavy and dull,

Smashes and bashes awful.

Unafraid of ogres,

Fighting them she does,

Gruesome eyes lovely, see skulls.

Grinds bones for meal,

When battle make hungry,

Thinking of her, then steam belly.

Meet Orc

Meet orc woman

Good

Talk nice to me

Not speak

Not share talk of her with orckind

She pretty

Must speak somehow though

so write here

write and not show, not show anyone

Tomorrow we talk again

and after I tell again what she like

tell again to page

Roses Red (1)

Roses are red,

Violets are blue,

All of them crush.

Transformation

It happen
a day with no-kill

Me not get mad MAD mAAaad

Instead,
dancing in flowers like an elf
prancy, prancy
axe nearby in case tribe find out

and flowers fill the air
pretty pretty flowers

Maybe one day turn into elf,
write big elf-poem

Pah, Elfsong!

Elfie poetry

lilting flow

Not understand

who can know?

Elfie poetry

smarty pride

Ork write stinky

but elfies died.

Adventuring Orc that Me

Not with rest of tribe to battle

Wander alone through elfie wood.

Pick pretty flower

Because must pick to make not pretty

and trees all shapen good, hack bad.

Elfie wood in general kept way too nice

Nice at all not what orc enjoy

Slash real bad that way to go.

Watch out for elfie

Hidden with bow

Could be end of wandering me.

But questing by self

Best way to hunt treasure

And gain expertise, become grand orc.

Burn

As to how it came about, that an Orc fought a book golem, likely it was the mad enchantress Vana Leissh who invented many ways to protect her collection of spell books from marauders. After the great fire from which some say Leissh found her own death, her arcane creations were found in settlements both human, orc, and throughout.

Burn burn burn
burn baby burn

That me thought on first seeing book golem
then think much better to rip
yaaarh! Rip!

Then me think
hm orc book

no

no orc book

no orc book yet

all the better reason to destroy book golem

all the smarty smarty books

probably elf book

Then get all toasty

and flint and steel

and what pretty smell all books aflame

Thinking afterward

like destroyed books

make room for new book

orc book

all my verse

and keep safe

no elf or human ruin

what of ogre

no ogre poetry

none ever

so I not allow, train, get strong, get good at melee

protect orc book also from ogre

Only Half Orc

Look at me

me half orc

human

I go there, they spit

human

say, "Leave us, you're not needed."

Except when needed

"Move this. Heft that for us. Kill that."

Then forgotten

human female

not like ugly

my ugly like most orc

my ugly my great horrible ugly--me--as beating heart in fist for this human female have no appreciation

except that one time

when girl like elfie flower descend on me

and think she thrash thrash, dream she thrash thrash

get all smiley-faced and not at all frowny

orcies like me

see me smart

help plan strategy

see more than once made successful bloodbath

but no one thrash like human girl

love orc

orc in me

orc home

orc smashings

but I like the way that human girl thrash

she show me about niceties, about pretties

human in me

weak side

it also smart side

at times it love side

but love side toward me hate

except that one time

Here and There

Here and there

Sword and bow

Keep steady

Come to human village

They strong in their own way

Dried meats at their store

Yes I pay, not growl and grab

I know some of their speak, the human tongue

Stay at their tavern, enjoy eats and drink

Human talk, like my hide

He show me sword, good blacksmithing, let him know I admire

But he not go kill like orc

He more use scythe in field

Not like me and mine

We not grow food, we take with sword

You know me traveling orc

Not marauding or war orc, like to see, like to write

See human, his kind

Get to think, could farm, could swing scythe with great orc arms

Live life say human, work dirt, make grow

He dream

But me traveling Orc

Not staying kind, not farm

My Whisper

Draw of the bow

like whisper

even as I crouch, pray like whisper to the blood-god

such delicate ears that elf, he not hear me, his bow at side.

blood-god hear me

hear my whisper, my blood

for all blood, earth, sky, you, me,

what elfies like, call pretty rain, it blood too

and with arrow I make blood

Pierce elf, he fall to knees,

second arrow

elf fall to ground

The others fire

and beginning of blood

one in my leg

Through his heart,

fourth arrow

another gone

There others still

but I write poem

who you think won?

In Secret

When so nice

me so nice

me no shout

me only show her weapon that she like

me promise to burn elf place for her

me not mash food

ok, mash a little

but not mash into her

that big improvement from last time

besides, some orc girl like food mashing.

You like, right?

I not know.

Someone like.

It hard not to mash food.

I bet she really mash food

in secret.

how an orc not mash food?

Blarrging Orc Poets!

I destroy you all!

You think I write poem!

You think I use this space to write poem!

You think!

You think!

You think!

Die!

Blood and Fire

small orc, great orc, strong orc

smash

we orc, she orc, flee orc

smash

blood run rivers

stony orc stand

northerner shivers

speak and command

life unchanging

war for father, war for children

ours is taking

setting rising sun

fires burn in our camps and into conquered towns

Crushes

Have crush

Get big club

Momma say all the time

You not crush girl

Yes Momma

Know Momma right

But what if girl also have crush?

I seen girl

And she have big club

Scared if I leave club at home

Could also be she want to see my club

Me only orc

Me not know

Today I meet girl

Find out

Coffee

It neat experience

far far away from orctown

coffee

nicey nice human brew

sure he look easy kill

surely have coppers

coffee

warm inside

belly feel it

sword remain in scabbard

there the secret of coffee

human share with me

the sword get tempting after cup run out

but when I wait human fill again

Coppers in Pocket

coppers for grub in human town
not silvers, not gold
those buy steel, those buy goods

merchant caravans
they carry more pretty coin
merchant caravans
guarded by heavies, warriors and magi

orc like me
not ready for those
take the straggler, the wanderer
and the coppers

coppers pay for grub
and grub will strengthen me

to take the next unfortunate on the road

maybe next will make me fortunate

win some chain, a sword, or gold coins

and strength and one day a caravan

Afar

Didn't think it ever happen to me

Female

across the far hills and past forest deep

Distance relationship

out with tribe

raiding caravans and human settlements

other tribes there, join in raid

she among them

only short time

compliment her on her fresh kill

catch her smile so full with sharp teeth

and away

not know

thoughts with me

not know

dreams with me

tribe home

resting, feasting

raiding season over

must I alone across far, past deep

Yah!

Great sword swing

Yah!

Great battle Orc

Yah!

think me so

enemies and tribe

Different inside

prefer pen

the kill, the loot

bold orcs

I live, I see

learn more, there something to know

there something to write

Sword draw blood

Better to draw ink

Do you know?

Finished poem

Toss pen, take sword

Eyes Not My Kind

Sylvan eyes, sylvan eyes
like stream, like swaying leaves
glittery cool like stars I sometime gaze

Though my bow is drawn
She has me
her eyes too much, my arms too weak
Far, far, in those eyes

In orc heart
    sense often, fire rage ready for kill
    red that boils over
    how cool, soft
    and knowing she can kill at ease
    her arrow notched, in elf eyes, death

Eyes meet eyes

she sees in me

blood murder, death upon death

lust and throttle, the evil of orc's love

as she ready-kill

again she sees

there another to this orc

it hurt

she take in breath, I take in breath

this orc a poet

it hurt

she lower bow and turn away eyes

see her back

feel my bow, feel my anger

watch her walk away

Can you share?

Can you hate and love?

my enemy's eyes

I cannot leave her eyes

Grog Night

froth sloshing
in our faces
in your face

smash a glass
in friend's jaw
and he smile
drink down brew

claw a girl
she bite on maw
growl and bite
grab forget all

years of grog
seven ago

that's how met wife

since then together

grog no more

Kill Dragon

Then there time we found dragon all asleep on treasure horde
me and family nine children and all
gather around and chop great lizard head to pieces
then sacks and sacks fill with gold

secret cave near the home village, there fill with gold
buy meats and mead
buy weapons and armor
best of every kind
buy and buy
and forget it all

back to simple life
plain orc family
kill and supper
and a fire by all

Roses Red (2)

Roses are red

Violets are blue

So is the enemy after he see you

Not that you are ugly

Not I don't want to see you

When you go to battle

I know your heart is true

Should you shake your head to know

Should you prove you are not beautiful

It's when we are together

You are for me and I am for you

we charge and smash

you no question me

because me: Master Strategist

Other ork question

He say he best strategist

Want to forward his strategy plan

no problem

he smashed and bashed

uncontested me

sole strategist

No Dice

dice! Diiiiiiiiiice!

lost my dice

bone dice

favorite dice

not your dice

now I borrow dice

when dead lie on the battlefield

we gather to gamble over loot

where are my dice?

are they spread on the field somewhere?

or lost on the day's march?

did I leave them in the mess among my saddle packs?

Look for dice?

or get new dice?

No Editor

sorry no editor

got hacked

remember him well

advice he gave before me got mad

bad like this

chop like that

rewrite

Rewrite!

that when I claw and bite and spit out his heart

too much rewrite

too much

too many hours on pages and pages

too much finishing and repairing

and ready with complete work

so no more editor

wonder what he say about my poem

Of Philosophy and Orc

start war

why war?

asked by human philosopher

what it good for?

good for no reason

also good for smash

no reason other than bash

see why human pose a hard philosophy

good: no reason

good: smash

How respond?

No reason and smash?

Stew human, answer to all human philosophy?

No, keep human around, his philosophy pretty smashing as well.

Roughness and Warts

Strong blooded female

roughness and warts

she club

I wake up happy

girl's arm around me

club at my side

Romance Female

Romance female; send poem

she club

I wake up happy

no girl,

no poem.

To See and Hear

Searing Heaven
close some days
calling close

the stink of a battle over
wading through that
parts of me left there
aside from blood

time amidst
to look, at times to see
friends and enemies gone that way
while I in the afterglory

"Closest to Heaven," he told me
Orc lying there

a quiet allowed the warrior after clashing steel

a heaven brought by ones who lie

"One day you join," say to me

Battle of Grog-Nor

Demon's blood

battle of Grog-Nor

Demon's blood

No one was ever same

Fighting elves and humans

usual bury the axe and claw the jaw

Other, else, not of

their kind neither ours

horror and ash

fell

bubbling of the air

seared skin

Those of us crawled off the field

left melted bodies there, elf, human, orc left care and worship

behind

Demon's blood

and no matter, no more elf, human, orc kind

Dreaming

Kill death

Slaarg battle slaughter

quiet on the road

dreaming, dreaming, dreaming

it not ork-like

it get misty dreamy

to look to stars above

to smile at little birdie

to love frost and tree

to dream of peace

Sharpened blade

to one day tame

Hard boots

to change for sandals

Rough leather armor

into clothing smooth

Murder Done

Got back from murder this eve

Last one

done

Left sword there.

Murder the name

Learned that from eloquent folk

Races not orc, not ogre, not troll

Peoples not scared

Got for quiet time

To be with brave folk

then talk

Some of them I kill, some not

With them I learned

Done with it

The blood-arm sick

The gold sack full

done

Go live on farm with brave peoples

Turn from sword to plough instead

Juicy Juicy Squishy Squish

Eyeballs squishy

yum yum yum

Eyeballs squishy

in the tum

Eyeballs squishy

In barrels all day

jump on the squishy

jump squirt juice

Jumping in the barrels

filled with eyes

jump jump jump

and eyeballs get juicy

keep on jumping

and good for juice

Bottling and bottling

lots of bottles

plenty of juice

for all orc party

and drink till burst!

Gevities

Elf live long, human live medium, orc live short.
That natural way, that normal way, that what elders say.

Better to slay the elf with all time in sun,
Human too with his chin proud, he think live longer than we orc.

Another way, besides live way
my way
way of orc
to cut
and I make cut into tradition way

To take long life
to take life of healthy
with proper mixture of fine grasses

with proper meditations on death-god

find life and strength

over those grown grim

for weakness in their bones

thereby I continue to trample well into old age

Kill Time

Enough kill time

anger brews in belly

Despite kill time

that usual makes me all right

Enough jaws broken

Enough throats crushed

Enough chests skewered

Enough bellies torn

Enough hip bones snapped

Still the wound within

That which does not bleed

That which can't be seen

Except by shape of my face

bodies lie contorted here

much my pain extroverted

tired of killing

tired of pain

carry my wound to next battle-day

Climb the Pyre

Climb the pyre
We fought on many field of war
and after in the grog hall
and I stood for him wedding day
now I climb his pyre

Times we raided
times we burned out fortifications
how he earned his fire
That I could stay, share with his last desire

now I leave to light the pyre
watch with tribe, wife and children
He takes his leave by wings of fire

Response to Dreaming

Solitude

a march at night

ten breadths from any ork

we skulkers

it ork, a dreaming

dream of death

dream of kill

it also ork-like to dream of other things

like grass we tread

stuck with thistles

and quiet mud

thick for slogging

Roses Red (3)

Roses red

Violets blue

diced with eyeballs

make for tasty stew

alternate end:

so good for you

Victory

(1)

Steady eyes can see

blood drained from this place

a field once red from battle

clean

swept of all anger

orcs about, none more to kill, no bodies even

elves, long since fled

in dread

and corpses lain here in times past, below earth

That time ago

I commanded my soldiers

we braved the elvish sword, elvish magic

seeming gentle kind brought death to many mine

This earth breathes
the young grow up without war
joy in their faces

(2)

My back aches
but I can still throw a spear

still lead orks to a charge
There is none

Remaining of my generation look to me as one who brought this,
The young look to me as hero of Brog-Narg-O
I walk among the peace fields composing words
limping for my wound by elf arrow
and wanting more
What of the charge? A matching elf arrow?

There will be no more

It is ours as far as eyes can see

Victory

Young Orc

As a young orc
Dream of leave village

Travel world
leave trail of broken hearts and broken heads
Conquer all that surrounds
out of dreams build Empire

That dreams of a young orc
the worn orc, the weathered orc
keeps dreams close to home

Path of destruction, woes and losses
much smaller than that dream
enjoy homebodies and pile of skulls

To Write Ugly

To write ugly

is true nature

Elfie writing

Gnomes of tricky burrows

Dwarves in glory for varieties of ore

humans in their ways

To be orc is to know

a blunt axe is all I need

The village is dirty

we would not clean if we had the time

life is short

and make short for others

Disease kill many our kind

as fine as battle-dead

our sickness kills enemy as well

pretty elf in victory so thought

as tender becomes rot

True nature

we bring

you wait, we bring ugly to you

Without Pen

Forgot pen today

that ok

write with bone

in elf-blood

Orker Orker

Yes me big writer

it big kill-season

all raiding party like

(1)

steady bow here

tribal friends with sword and toothed axe

me kneel with bone blood

scholar, scholar, book ork

in fields around still elves to kill

Orker Orker

Me want you know

me not coward

hide here writing in elf-blood

should elf arrow interrupt writing

me go kill

Orker Orker

Worse if tribal finds me

then kill me

ork yell, ork kill

see me make you understand

me write

write brave

time and battle and ork and elf-blood not be lost, me save

with pen

Orker Orker

(2)

me write

Anthropological Notes:

all raiding party like

(1) It is unclear whether the Ork is referring to himself here, or the raid. It is doubtful that the poet is using a double meaning here because that would be too 'smarty' too 'elfie.' It may be that the sentence is made intentionally unclear so as to imply to the reader that the poet is not intelligent enough to write with clarity.

Orker Orker

(2)

This appears to be a technique in Orkish poetry. The

poet may have demanded that no other ork follow in kind; the poet may have even destroyed other works and other poets to prevent such. So far there is no confirmed use of this technique.

Pomarj Days

O Pomarj days

when we were younger

O Pomarj days

of smite and plunder

O Pomarj days

where cleave asunder

On Pomarj days

should elfies wander?

Die by axe or sword or gnaw?

My father oft preferred the claw

Either way into no more

Magic blooded elves amighty

Slendery skills with bows and pretty swords

Orken hordes charge, turn them afrighty

Flighty flighty elves

whispy whispy

on dinner fires o so crispy

O Pomarj days

of yesterday's thunder

O Pomarj days

give cleft to wonder

On Pomarj days

slaid sylvan kin when we were younger.

Today no longer do that. Let boys and girls play with elf-bones, and turn in fire. Was that meat I seen in fire? Some of those ork children getting big, pretty good with spear and club. Maybe playing with elf corpse.

Tired Me Write

50 poems

Tired me write

No more war

With sword, with pen

No more war

A'weary me is

No fight for more

You want me fight or write?

You wait for war.

Thrat—Thrat!

Bat—a—Bat—a—tum—tum

War!

To War!

Bat—a—Bat—a—tum—tum

March!

To March!

Thrash the enemy tum—tum

Through them march

through them slash right past their line

Bat—a—Bat—a—smash—smash

Their throats cut

they think they strong

fingers aflying
they think they hold sword

Like to bite off their ear
like to tear out their tongue
gouge their ribcage make drum

All lying, all death
view carnage, great carpet
quiet overlook, me master

Back home and soup from their bones
Drumstick, drumstick
Bat—a—Bat—a—tum—tum

Bye Bye Elfie

Elfie Elfie
flower and tree
leaf and rosy
unlike me

Gnash and smash
tear with claw
bite and bite
until bony raw

Elfie Elfie
you so tremble
with every look
it too easy
to write refined book

Once marauding

weapons known well

put up no fight

slaying I tell

Elfie Elfie

trouble me no more

your quiver run out (your pen run dry)

you dead by my sword

Dear my Elfie

why you not gone yet?

already I have you

splattered meaty wet

Hallowed Ground

Blood and snot and sweat and saliva
Hallowed ground, Hallowed ground
Battlefield, battle-death

Clawing through those fluids
is afterlife reached
To breathe congealed of war
holy honor
Survivors see dead who earned a place by such rage

To be hacked
To be spread across the field
friend and enemy intermingled
Such sharing, bonding, a togetherness that takes us into next world

Odorous Times

Oh revelous reek

Ode to odor

Ode to smell

battle of stinky corpses

feet of fetid march

snot root odor of divided flavor

war paint of smelly plant that blended with mud

These times

These smells

Rotty gut fishy gut

On a raid, smash a barrely fishy, eat them raw, go aswim in scaly

Claw open and mash about face

Grab tail and whack friend fish guts spewing

Oh stinky time

For love with nostrils entwined

Sock sweat ale

Finest stench

Compounded by letting in bucket for months

To keg of alchoholly sweat

Stinky drunk

Ambrosial passion

Bravery Meaning

Acry among the battle dead

The smashed and the bashed

It no good

In bravery me say that

For love

That long in my heart

No matter the kill

No matter the taste of the dead

In heart

Feel for my love

She not know my inside softness

These of none orc know

Know what? Not know

Yelling from mine kind

For limbs ascatterd and heads arolled

But they not know

You not know

What Dream May Come

What dream may come

for savage bloodlust

born to rife of snot and blood

I leave tribe

What can lone Orc do

lone wanting more than that?

So hard to reach, to dream

How even I get here from rust and dust?

Give up kill innocent

Give up eating manbone

Look astrange me

They say

pondkiller

snakefriend

aleduller

unto me

To look up, to become

that life, best chooser

even for groundy

dream me

dream me

This book was written in the city of San Diego among others in the following places:

Lestat's cafe

Infusions of Tea

Starbucks

17410651R10064

Made in the USA
Charleston, SC
10 February 2013